What Shapes an Ape?

WHAT SHAPES AN APE?

A RED FOX BOOK 0 09 943864 X

Published in Great Britain by Red Fox,
an imprint of Random House Children's Books

This edition published 2002

1 3 5 7 9 10 8 6 4 2

Red Fox Books are published by Random House Children's Books,
61–63 Uxbridge Road, London W5 5SA,
a division of The Random House Group Ltd,
in Australia by Random House Australia (Pty) Ltd,
20 Alfred Street, Milsons Point, Sydney, NSW 2061, Australia,
in New Zealand by Random House New Zealand Ltd,
18 Poland Road, Glenfield, Auckland 10, New Zealand,
and in South Africa by Random House (Pty) Ltd,
Endulini, 5A Jubilee Road, Parktown 2193, South Africa

THE RANDOM HOUSE GROUP Limited Reg. No. 954009
www.kidsatrandomhouse.co.uk

A CIP catalogue record for this book is available from the British Library.

Printed in Hong Kong by Midas Printing Limited

What Shapes an Ape?

Gina Douthwaite

RED FOX

CONTENTS

What Shapes an Animal?

Not-So Animal Antics

ANiMaL FRiGHtS

MaN aNd ANiMaL

WHAT SHAPES AN ANIMAL?

INFLAMMABLE CAMEL

is an **animal** A **camel**
so inflammable with temper
ed with immense it must be treat-
and haughti- respect. Its arrogance
naughtiness ness turn quickly into
could well when cloven hooves, and you,
thump a camel, it would take the hump at
any such attempt to make it stand, and
spit, without a hint of charm, then sink
its teeth into your arm and drag you
off across the desert sand, sand
sand **sand** sand sand
sand **sand** sand sand
sand **sand** sand sand
sand **sand** sand sand
sand sand sand sand
sand sand sand sand
sand sand sand sand
sand **sand** sand
sand **sand** sand
sand sand sand sand
sand **sand** sand sand
sand sand
...

SiX O'CLOCK FOX

Cop-
per coat
ablaze, tail brushing stubble, he stalks,
pauses . . . picking paws he pricks signal ears,
directs wet pebble eyes beyond his
twitch of whiskers. Freeze-framed, he
holds   the   moment,   then sweeps
t o   streak   towards
the   swell-
ing   sun.

White Horses

White
horses are
charging on top
of the
waves,
galloping
shoreward
to crash into
caves, surge over rocks on
in a fury of foam, rear
their hocks in a
stinging of spume.
Snorting ashore
on a steep,
shingle strand,
white horses,
exhaust-
ed, seep
into
the
sand.

NeW SHoeS

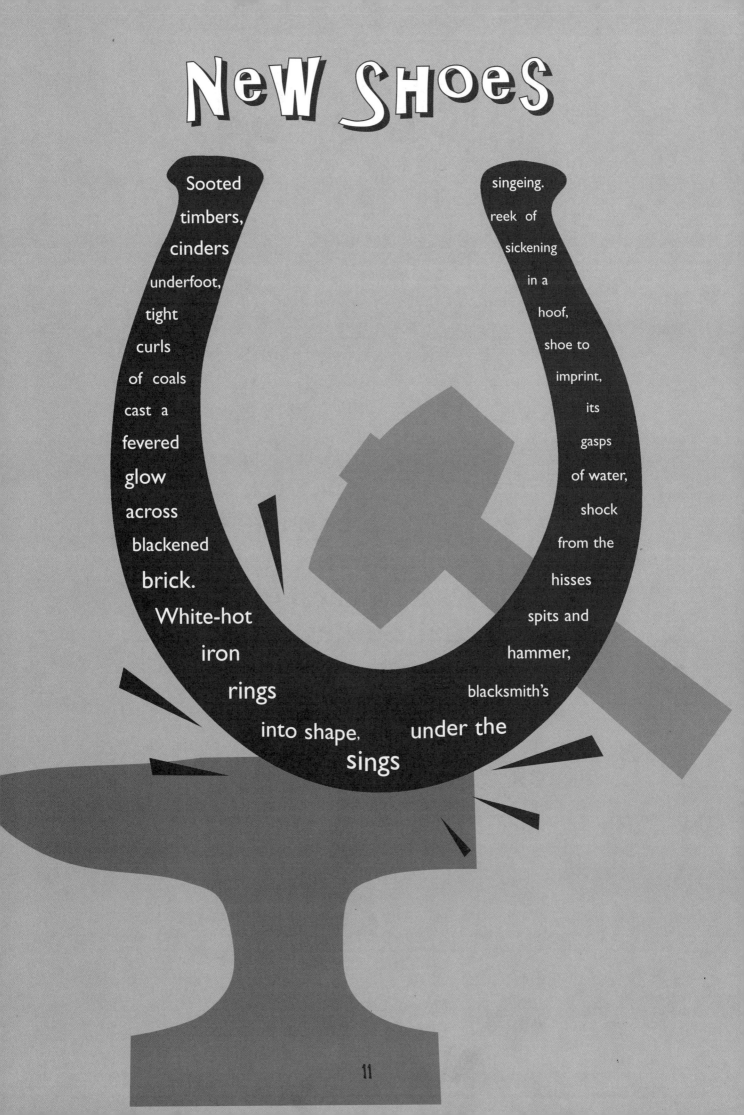

Sooted timbers, cinders underfoot, tight curls of coals cast a fevered glow across blackened brick. White-hot iron rings into shape, sings under the blacksmith's hammer, spits and hisses from the shock of water, gasps its imprint, shoe to hoof, in a sickening reek of singeing.

Nick's Cat

Slick
cat
quick cat,
flick a bit
o' stick cat,
chase a ghost of rat cat,
make a nest of
mat cat, curl up
in a hat cat, lick
a coat that's thick
cat – sick cat. Nick's cat.

SynonyMouse With Spring

Mouse
in a hedge
scurrieS
up a twig,
leaps like
a lion
brave and big,
clings to a leaf
that's spinning
round and round,
mouse in a hedge is
dizzy off the ground,
drops into daffodils,
ripples through the
grass, scurries up
a twig again.

S
p
r
i
n
g
a
t
l
a
s
t.

Mined by Moles

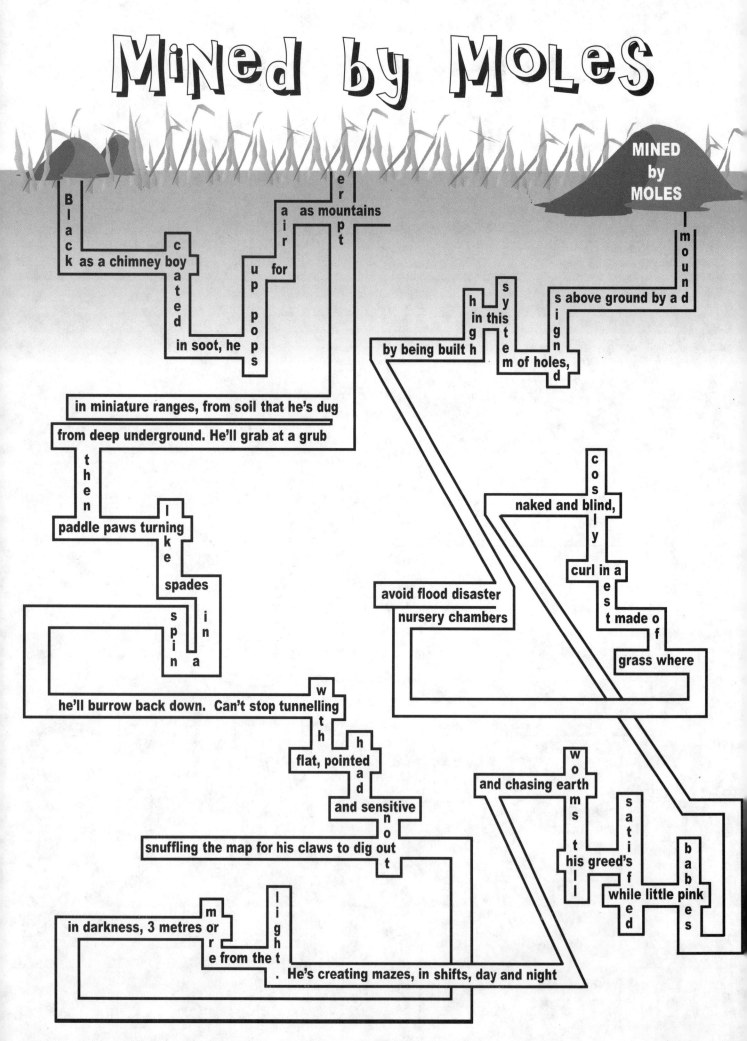

Black as a chimney boy coated in soot, he up pops air as mountains erupt for in miniature ranges, from soil that he's dug from deep underground. He'll grab at a grub then paddle paws turning like spades spin in a spin he'll burrow back down. Can't stop tunnelling with flat, pointed head and sensitive snout snuffling the map for his claws to dig out in darkness, 3 metres or more from the light. He's creating mazes, in shifts, day and night and chasing earthworms till his greed's satisfied while little pink babes naked and blind, cosily curl in a nest made of grass where high in this system of holes, signs above ground by a mound avoid flood disaster nursery chambers by being built

MINED
by
MOLES

Muddy Mongrel

One
paw
two paws
three paws
four
thousand
paw marks
on the
floor.

PHeaSant

Pheasant **strutting** like a lord in green-sheen *balaclava*, trying to attract a mate so he can be a father, flicks his tick of yellow eye, displays hides pride behind a mask, his vicar's collar in this mixed-up-matching task. He preens red, pencilled feathers, shakes shavings from his back and points a scaly leg as though he's ready to attack the dull, brown bird he's spotted but greets her with a cry that's like a throttled engine that's threatening to die. She turns away, this dull brown bird, plays hard-to-get which brings a ruffle to his plumage, a clockwork whir of wings, a launching of his mind — divided body, a tearing of his as his **airborne** tail as he leaves her behind.

MiLKiNG TiMe

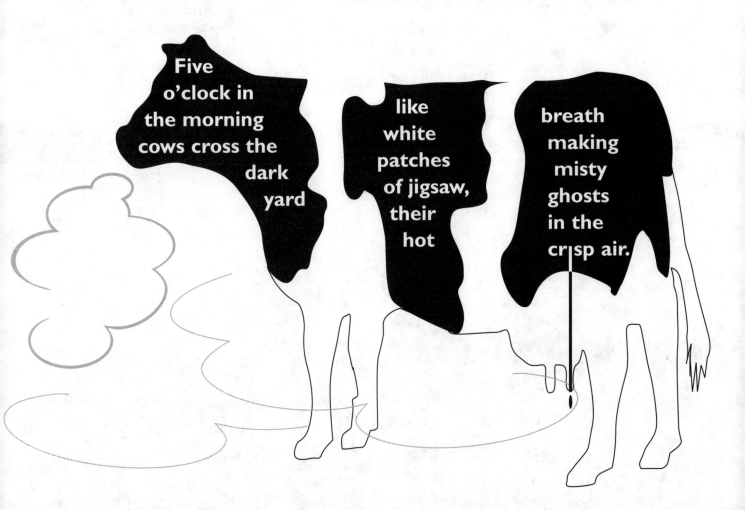

Five o'clock in the morning cows cross the dark yard

like white patches of jigsaw, their hot

breath making misty ghosts in the crisp air.

RHiNOS and ROSeS

When more than one rhinoceros becomes rhinoceroses, and each of these has horns of hair that stick up from their noses, and armoured skin that wallows in the mud when they reposes, and on each foot each rhino has three hooves instead of toeses—the features of these creatures show the problem language poses when more than one rhinoceros becomes rhinoceroses.

PURE NEW WOOL

On legs ten sizes too big
head-butt the pole that grows
newly knit lambs
from their hillside.

In a lamb gang they practise being rams
then spring, like Jacks-from-boxes, and scatter in a clockwork dash
to head-butt a milky mum.

19

Step by Step

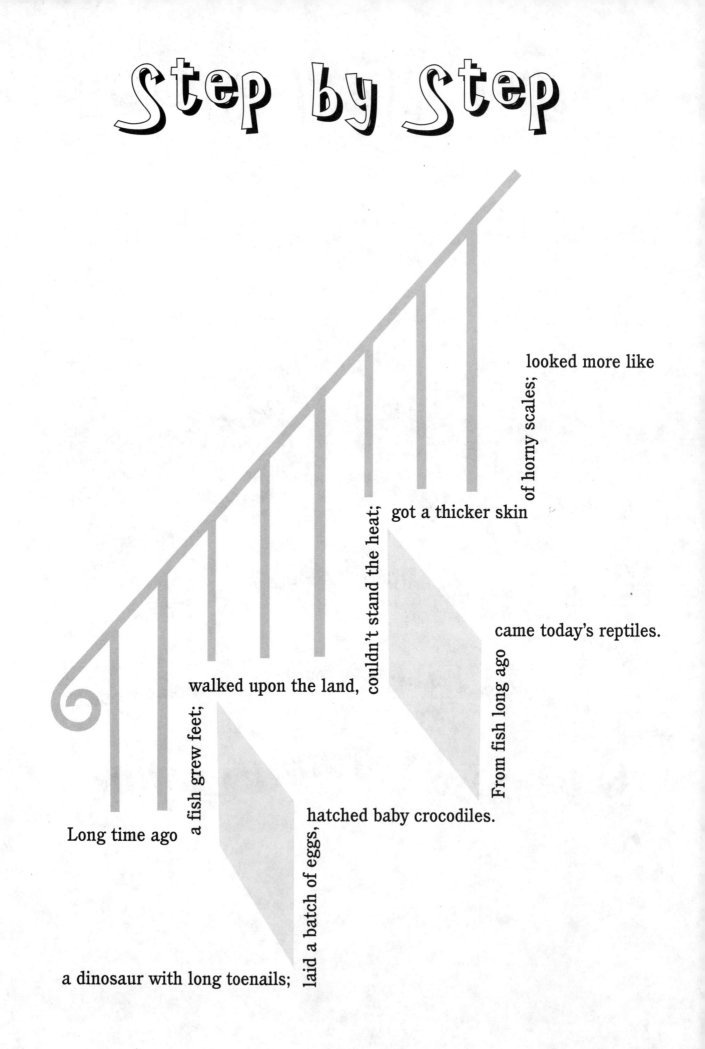

looked more like

of horny scales;

got a thicker skin

couldn't stand the heat;

came today's reptiles.

walked upon the land,

From fish long ago

a fish grew feet;

hatched baby crocodiles.

Long time ago

laid a batch of eggs,

a dinosaur with long toenails;

What Shapes an Ape?

An
ape is
the
shape
of a
man
with a
great,
big
weight
on his   shoulders,
with lollop-   ing gait; a
man with long arms —
like man's lies they have
stretched. An ape
grasps at branches with muscles well-flexed as
man grabs at chances, then moves to the next. An
ape will behave like a man with a brain
that's half in the dark as a
moon on the wane: it
chatters and chunters
and grumbles
through teeth,
like man in the
morning, and scratches
beneath the hair it is spawning.
There's long-held belief that from early
ape came superior beings: intelligent, gentle,
with sensi-   tive feelings, considerate
creatures   related to
man — the
chimp, the
gorilla
a n d
orang-
utan.

Not-So Animal Antics

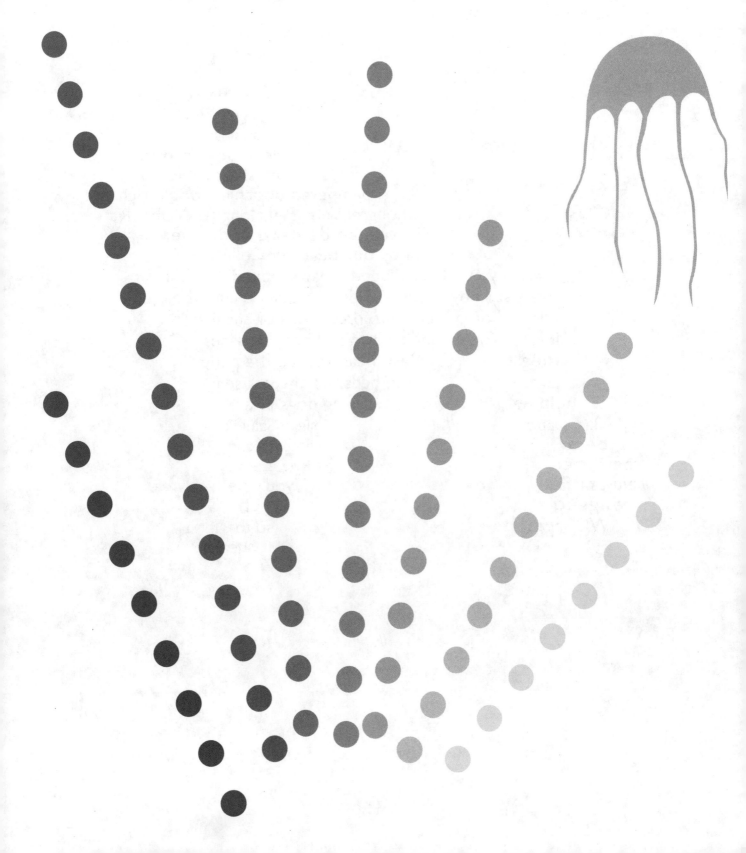

It's a Dog's Life

Book at
WUFTER's for
a hairdo, cut and
blow-dry, trim or
tint, shaggy stray or
pampered poochie, poodle rich or
mongrel skint. Pad along to WUFTER's
parlour, be de-flea'd upon the
couch by our Bearded Collie, Carla.
Have your claws clipped – paws nipped, OUCH!
Try a style by Snippy Whippet, coats are curled or
crimped or combed into dreadlocks or she'll strip
it like a Greyhound's, down to bone. Massages by
Meg the Mastiff can reduce the puppy
fat, saunas, sun beds, are the last sniff –
helping working dogs relax.
Be a supple, sleek Saluki,
be a preened and
perfumed Peke, whether
Mutt or Fido you'll be
wagged with
WUFTER's, so to
speak.

24

BUMCONUNDRUM

I saw a thing that landed on
what must have been
its sit-upon
and
there it sat

until it stood and hid itself
inside a hood. I went to look, to say, 'Hello',
knocked on its head, which made it go
with such a blast! Yet, what a find...

its   sit-upon

was   left

behind.

Sucker

A limpet lost a leg or two, dancing on the rocks, his crusty crab and lobster friends and three old crayfish crocks were not impressed by limpet's limp. It had upset their rhythm. 'Go jump into a pool,' they moaned. He did – but can't forgive 'em for on a rock his one last foot got stuck, as if concreted and now he sits inside his shell, alone, limp and defeated.

Bird Brain

An Ostrich from Ipswich was itching and scratching, and stretching his neck for a flea needed catching. He swivelled around so his head and beak pointed right back where he'd come from, contorted, disjointed. He poised and prepared to attack but the flea leapt out from his feathers, acrobatic'ly, and looped through the air like a stunt aeroplane. The ostrich looped too, without using his brain

– his neck got con-
torted and tied in a
knot, so tightly
that from
that day
ostrich for-
got just every- thing!
From the
neck up
he was
blank, not
even remember-
ing a flea
was to thank.

DUCKWeeD DaiLy

BIRThS

WEBFOOT

To Drip (née Mudwet) and Flapper, at Duckend Maternity Nest on April 1st, twin eggs. Both cracked.

MARRIAGES

WEBFOOT-WADDLE

Mr and Mrs F. Webfoot of Lakeside wish to announce the marriage of their twin daughter Puddle to Shaky, 10th son of Mr and Mrs Q. Waddle of Waterstown. The wedding will take place at Ditchbottom Chapel at dawn on Saturday, followed by a reception at the Stagnant Pond Hotel.

DEAThS

WADDLE

Puddle, dear wife of Shaky. By accident. The funeral will be held on Squashy Corner, at rush hour. Donations please, in aid of Duck Safety, to the lollipop lady.

Rest in Reeds.

Abracaboa

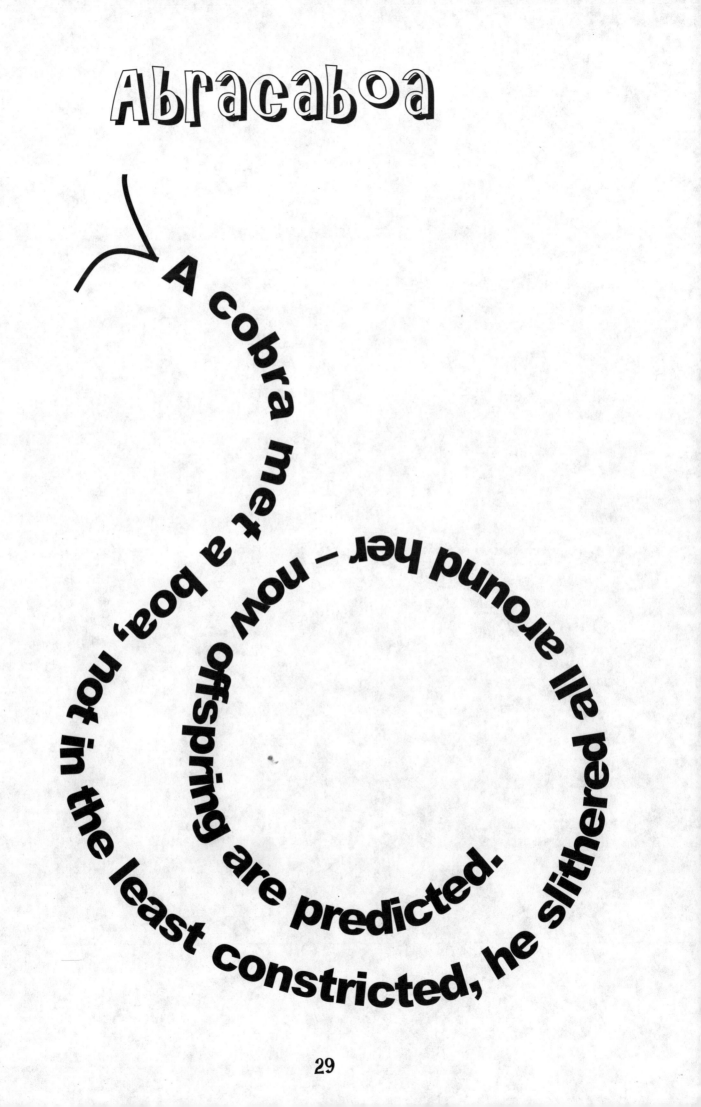

A cobra met a boa, not in the least constricted, he slithered all around her – now offspring are predicted.

AN ACCOUNT OF a Centipede

Do not impede a centipede who's doing his accounts,

he counts on legs so losing count could make an odd amount

but losing legs and counting counts could more confuse his balance.

If centipedes can't calculate then one must make allowance.

Hydropod Slob

Ten tentacles like tyre tracks
wrapped round her mollusc waist. 'Relax,'
the Hydropod slobbed in her ear,
'lie back upon the sea bed, dear,
and I'll fish-kiss your frilly lips,

I'll feed you ocean-ready chips
and stroke your silky, see-through gills
for floating here with you gives thrills
like tidal waves ... Oh! Molly, please
don't go into your shell. Don't tease!'

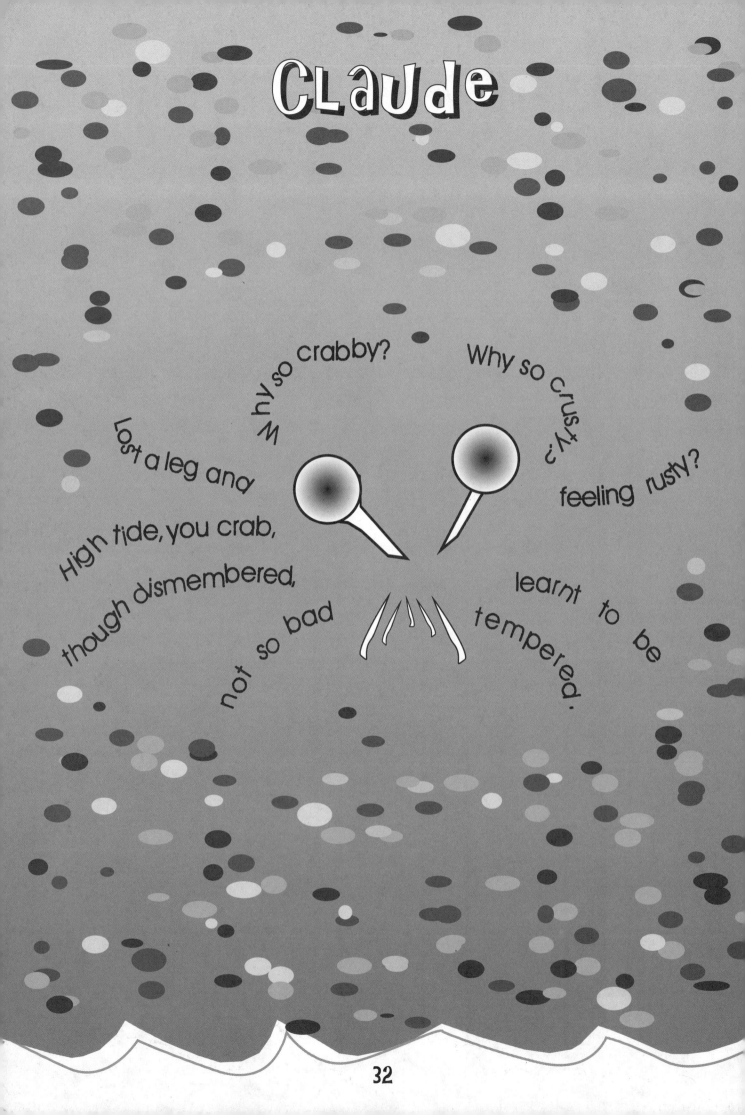

CLaUde

Why so crabby? Why so crusty? feeling rusty?

Lost a leg and

High tide, you crab,

though dismembered,

not so bad

learnt to be

tempered.

SNOUT DOING

Said Hedgehog to Badger, 'Oh, let's marry, do-
we'll shickle and pruffle and sup hogger stew,
we'll insect each other with liCe evermore,
have badgehogs in batches and hedgers galoree,
We'll live so snuffit twogether as one,
till we

Said Badger to Hedgehog, 'Oh, fleas run along,
I do get your point but I'm sett in my ways
and thoroughly sick of rollmantic displays
so don't take a fence, Hedge, but this is my plot-
just go hog a headlight and badger me not.'

SHELLFISH CONTEST

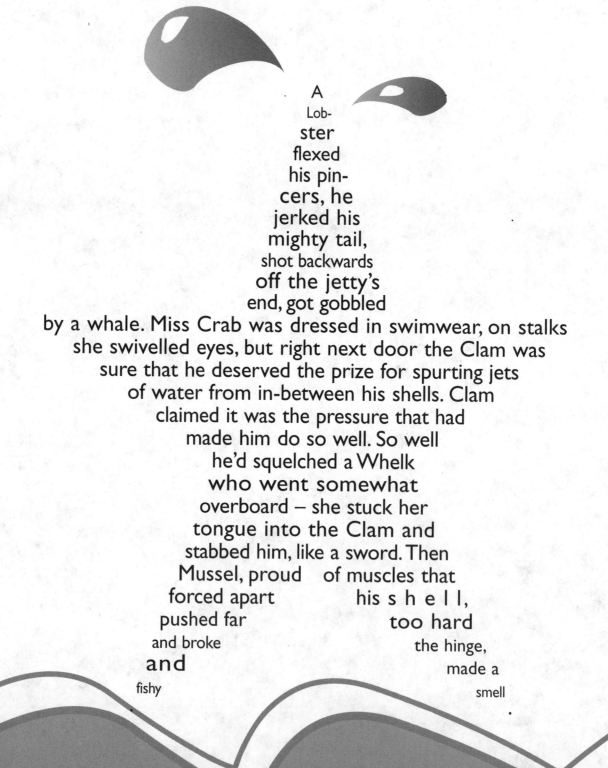

A
Lob-
ster
flexed
his pin-
cers, he
jerked his
mighty tail,
shot backwards
off the jetty's
end, got gobbled
by a whale. Miss Crab was dressed in swimwear, on stalks
she swivelled eyes, but right next door the Clam was
sure that he deserved the prize for spurting jets
of water from in-between his shells. Clam
claimed it was the pressure that had
made him do so well. So well
he'd squelched a Whelk
who went somewhat
overboard – she stuck her
tongue into the Clam and
stabbed him, like a sword. Then
Mussel, proud   of muscles that
forced apart   his s h e l l,
pushed far   too hard
and broke   the hinge,
and   made a

fishy   smell

It drift- ed to his neigh- bour, a spiky Ur- chin who was preening spines so perk- ily until she smelt it, too. Prawn, blushing pretty pinkish, cracked up, could not perform, stood shell-shock stiff when his turn came and wished he'd not been born, so hid behind the Cockle who wailed, 'You silly *Pidd—', before he cockled in the sea, and Prawn was glad he did, for though the Prawn was spine-less and clearly was a wimp, he puffed with pride, was chuffed, wide eyed, to watch his cousin, Shrimp, change shape into a starfish, outshining all, by far. 'The Best Shell- fish', without a doubt, was Shrimp. He was a ★.

* Cockle was about to say, 'You silly Piddock!'

ALligator Waiter

Alligator Waiter waited patiently, at fat Mabel's table, took her home for tea, hated, achingly scraping scraps of Mabel from his clock. Alligator ate her, ery. ∨∨∨ ∨∨∨

THE POTAMUSLESS

A hippopotamus
once lost his pota on a bus,
not noticing until he was dropped
at the terminus, where he alighted, lighter
than he'd been when he'd got on. And looking back he realized that his mus had also
gone. That's how the Potamus-   less came
about, hip-hippo-ray! 'Twas   when the

hippo-   potamus
the bus,   that   day.

rode on

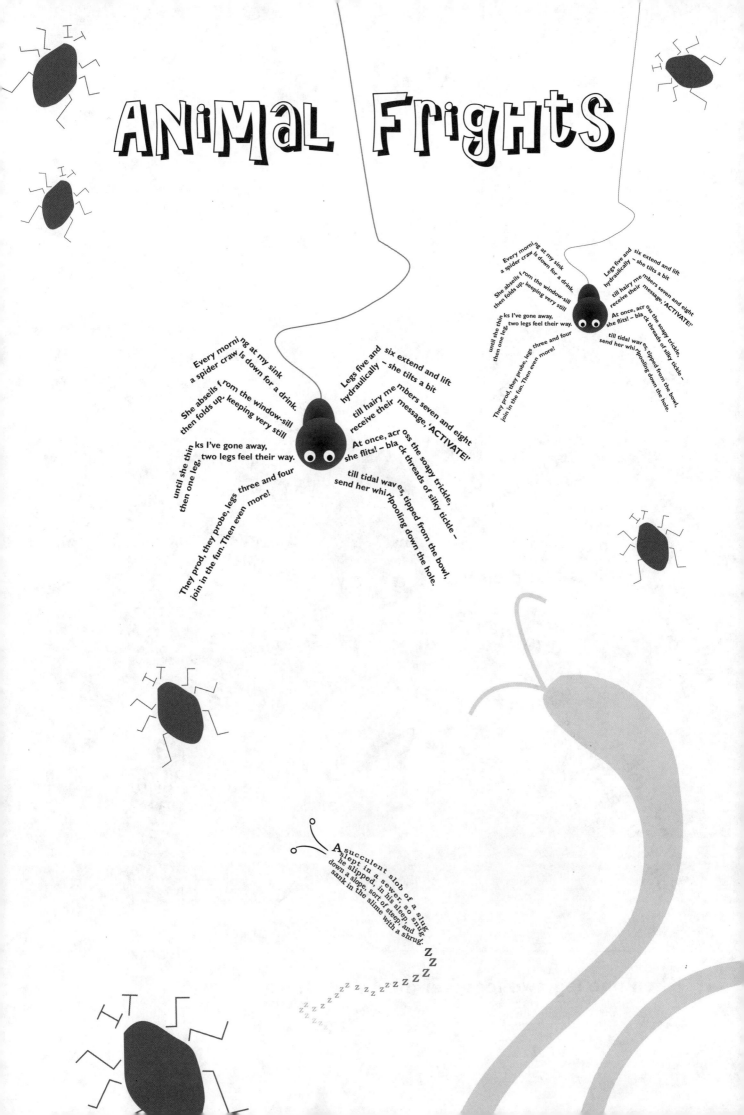

ANiMal FrightS

Every morning at my sink
a spider crawls down for a drink.
She abseils from the window-sill
then folds up, keeping very still

until she thinks I've gone away,
then one leg, two legs feel their way.

They prod, they probe, legs three and four
join in the fun. Then even more!

Legs five and six extend and lift
hydraulically – she tilts a bit
till hairy members seven and eight
receive their message, 'ACTIVATE!'

At once, across the soapy trickle,
she flits! – black threads of silky tickle –

till tidal waves, tipped from the bowl,
send her whirlpooling down the hole.

Every morning at my sink
a spider crawls down for a drink.
She abseils from the window-sill
then folds up, keeping very still

until she thinks I've gone away,
then one leg, two legs feel their way.

They prod, they probe, legs three and four
join in the fun. Then even more!

Legs five and six extend and lift
hydraulically – she tilts a bit
till hairy members seven and eight
receive their message, 'ACTIVATE!'

At once, across the soapy trickle,
she flits! – black threads of silky tickle –

till tidal waves, tipped from the bowl,
send her whirlpooling down the hole.

A succulent slob of a slug
slept in a sewer, so snug;
he slipped, in his sleep,
down a slope, sort of steep, and
sank in the slime with a shrug.

Z
Z
Z
Z Z Z Z Z Z Z Z Z Z Z Z Z Z Z Z Z Z Z Z

Spider

Every morning at my sink
a spider crawls down for a drink.

She abseils from the window-sill
then folds up, keeping very still

until she thinks I've gone away,
then one leg, two legs feel their way.

They prod, they probe, legs three and four
join in the fun. Then even more!

Legs five and six extend and lift
hydraulically – she tilts a bit

till hairy members seven and eight
receive their message, 'ACTIVATE!'

At once, across the soapy trickle,
she flits! – black threads of silky tickle

till tidal waves, tipped from the bowl,
send her whirlpooling down the hole.

Then one leg, two legs feel their way . . .

40

Bathroom Bug

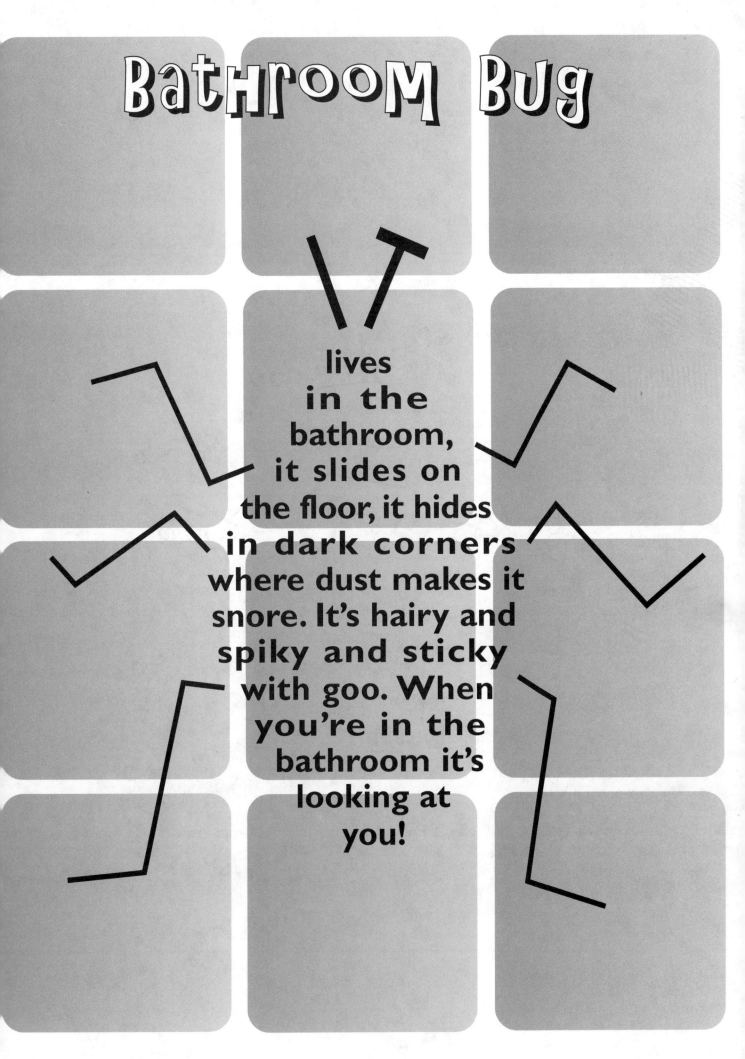

lives
in the
bathroom,
it slides on
the floor, it hides
in dark corners
where dust makes it
snore. It's hairy and
spiky and sticky
with goo. When
you're in the
bathroom it's
looking at
you!

COOLING POOLS

Green and greasy, muddy puddles, with a crust of scum and slime, stinking like decaying cabbage, to a dog are quite divine.

Rat Castles

Rats
on crackly castles
built of bales of straw
jump   up to the battlements, leap and
loop, explore the tickliest of tunnels, play
chasing through a maze of thickly prickly passages
and   giant-step stairways.   In fields across the
country,   where winds play
                                      stubble's tune,
                                rats   celebrate   in
                                                            c
                                                          a
                                                        s
                                                        t
                                                          l
                                                            e
                                                            s
                                                            b
                                                          e
                                                        n
                                                        e
                                                          a
                                                            t
                                                              h
                                                            e
                                                          t
                                                        h
                                                        a
                                                          r
                                                            v
                                                              e
                                                              s
                                                            t
                                                          m
                                                        o
                                                        o
                                                          n
                                                            .

Barn Owl

Hunched
under
Hood

his Killer's
cloak, claws
hooked on wood,
he cocks his
love-heart head,
glints sapphire
eyes as neat-
beak sharp as
the swoop,
the screech,
the death.

ISLAND DINO

I see an
island in the sea.
It's like a dinosaur. Its sleepy
eye of sun awakes as I watch
from the shore. Its rocky back is
rough and black upon its bed of waves.
It yawns a hungry warning to the fishes in
its caves, then lumbers up on lumpy legs – its
frilly socks start slipping round its ankles as it wades,
stumbl-   ing and tripping, from the sea   bed,
where   it's slept a mill-   ion
years   or more.   And
only I   have seen
it wake – my
island
dinosaur.

MiSter MyTHOLOGy

Mister
Mythol**O**gy's
got a
dead
head

with ammonite eyes that don't blink.
He lies at the mouth of his cave,
every dawn, to peck leather
feathers and think, about
finding bones for
his breakfast.
His beak,

practising taps on old boulders,
crumbles away like a climbed cliff of chalk.
The weight on Mythology's
shoulders is shifted
to stand on one
fish-scaly
leg,

with tin wings
that have never
flown, he raps at
his chest in its
grey armoured
vest
and

s
c
r
a
t
c
h
e
s

h
i
s
/
s
t
o
r
y

in stone.

46

Dreaded Dribbler

Scary
and hairy with
huge, huggy limbs,
hungry to get me it spins and
it spins, rushes and gushes, rolls
over the top, squeezes me, teases
me, wish ● it would ● stop
pressing   itself on the window   behind,
flipping   its fingers. It's   mad in
its   mind, throwing   and
thrash-   ing and try-   ing
to   get in, flapping
and slapping
and

d-

r

i

b-

b-

l

i

n

g.

SLUGGISH

A succulent slob of a slug
slept in a sewer, so snug,
he slipped, in his sleep,
down a slope, sort of steep, and
sank in the slime with a shrug.

Z Z Z z z z z z z z z z z z z z z z z z z

48

Vet's Surgery

Yap and squawk and yowl and growl,
grunt and oink, miaow,
flap and bawl and howl and scowl.
Who brought in that cow?

Treated toad for diarrhoea.
Plastered bone. Stitched rat's ripped ear.
Bandaged badger's poorly paw.
Soothed a horse's saddle sore.
Gave the kiss of life to fish.
Shampooed hamster (ticklish!).
Sold worm tablets to a worm.
Poked a pig to kill a germ.
Put a pigeon's wing in splints.
Cured a cockatoo of squints.
Kissed a kangaroo with lumps
(leans lopsided when he jumps).

Yap and squawk and yowl and growl,
grunt and oink, miaow,
flap and bawl and howl and scowl.
Who brought in that cow!

MaN and ANiMaL

Captivating or Captive Creature

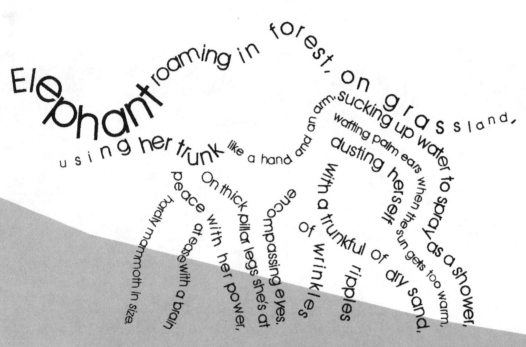

Elephant roaming in forest, on grassland,
using her trunk like a hand and an arm,
sucking up water to spray as a shower,
wafting palm ears when the sun gets too warm,
dusting herself with a trunkful of dry sand,
With a trunkful of dry sand,
Of wrinkles
With a trunkful of ripples
encompassing eyes.
On thick pillar legs she's at
peace with her power,
at ease with a brain
hardly mammoth in size

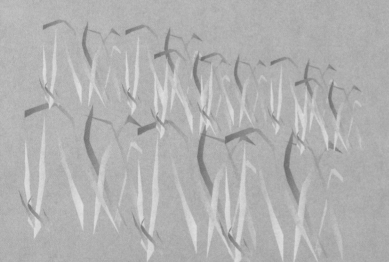

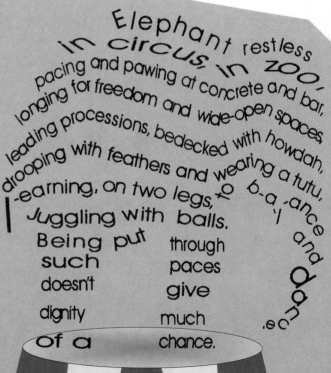

Elephant restless in zoo,
in circus,
pacing and pawing at concrete and bar,
longing for freedom and wide-open spaces.
leading processions, bedecked with howdah,
drooping with feathers and wearing a tutu,
-earning, on two legs, to b-a-l-ance and dance.
Juggling with balls.

Being put   through
such   paces
doesn't   give
dignity   much
of a   chance.

Never Laugh at a Giraffe

D.
on't ever
laugh at a
giraffe in his jig-
saw
jacket,
he
couldn't
hide so
well in
trees, if
he didn't
have it. And
never giggle at his
neck or snigger at
his tongue, it's not
as though he asked
for them to be so
very long. And please
don't mimic his stiff legs as
they splay into splits – he's
very conscious of the way it's
awkward for these bits to
get themselves positioned
so that he can have a drink.
He knows he's looking
clum-   sy   but don't
laugh   at   him, just
think   of   what he
feels   when   looking
at   your   squashed
and   shrunken   shape   that's
chittering   and gaping,   like an idiotic ape.

Debra Zebra

Now, Debra the zebra
was bright, being stripeless,
her rarity value
indelibly priceless.

One night she was rustled
away from the park
by thieves who thought that they
were safe in the dark.

But they were as thick as
Deb's decor was thin,
for Debra was spotted,
all white in her skin.

Why?

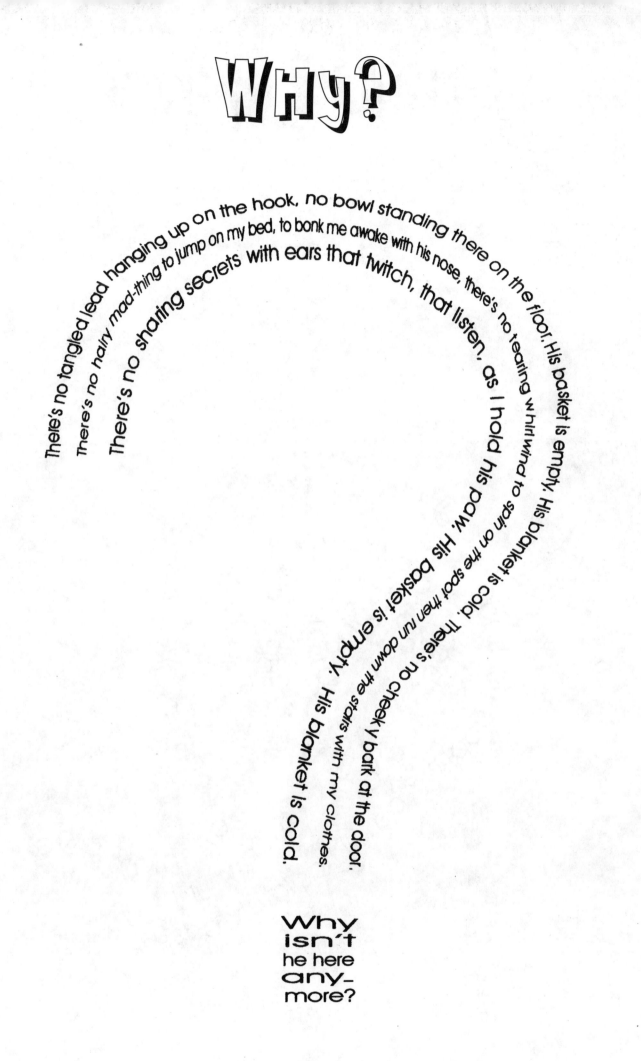

There's no tangled lead hanging up on the hook, no bowl standing there on the floor. His basket is empty. His blanket is cold. There's no tearing whirlwind to spin on the spot then run down the stairs with my clothes. His blanket is cold.

There's no hairy mad-thing to jump on my bed, to bonk me awake with his nose, there's no cheeky bark at the door.

There's no sharing secrets with ears that twitch, that listen, as I hold his paw. His basket is empty. His blanket is cold.

Why
isn't
he here
any-
more?

SNAIL'S PACE

snail's caravan, caved-in, crushed, no longer can move upon its shoe of glue to leave a tell-tale trail, a clue of shiny silver that would say— a snail has lately passed this way.

WiLD Bear Tame Bear
(can it be the same bear?)

Bears in the bushes, bears in the trees, bears on other bears picking off fleas. Bears killing seals, bears killing rivers, fish. Bears gobbling grass and leaves, and frogs and mice eating bears.

Bears bleeding from wounds, bears in a circus, bears wearing chains, bears bearing blisters, dancing in pain, bears biting other bears, begging food bears, begging food bears in prison pits, bears in...

Blackbird

Black-bird. Dead. Dumped in a bin. Your life has been taken. It seems such a sin. Did you fly at a window that mirrored a tree? Not everything is what it's seen to be.

EXPERIMENT IN PUPPY LOVE

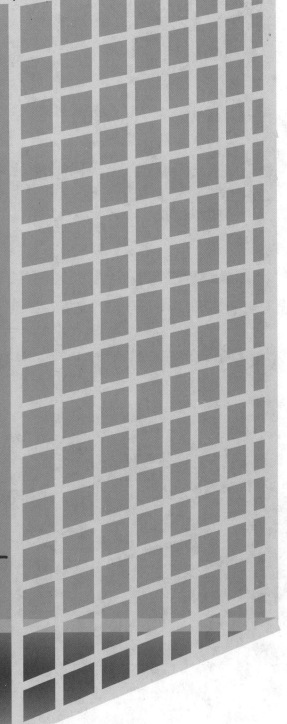

I've never snuggled on a lap,
I've never had a cuddle
nor stretched out in the sunshine
nor paddled in a puddle.

I've never sniffed a blade of grass,
I've never gnawed a bone
nor curled up by a fireside
nor chased a stick or stone.

I've never walked upon a lead,
I've never had a name
nor known a home beyond this cage –
just needles, fear and pain.

Freedom

At the first swathe of dawn
dogs wag and scramble
in a clockwork frenzy,
rummage in a slung wigwam
of twig and branch
scenting rabbit,
fox and mouse.

In this fractured wood
where ripped roots
reach like snakes from the graves of trees,
two deer,
mottled by morning,
appear.

Their presence drifts on a wave of breeze . . .
dogs freeze.
Then dart!

Deer break,
crash through sapless scrub . . .
one,
with rider-less grace,
clears the hedge and is gone.

The other bounds uncertainly
then sets herself into the rising sun,
its ray a pathway pulling up the hill.
This way! This way!

Dogs chase.
Gain ground.
She turns
and black, in miniature,
heaves beneath the halo of the day.

One way remains to win this race –
with instinct sharpened from the wild
she gambles theirs is man-made blunt
and stands
to call
her hunters' bluff . . .

In one, four-legged leap
she's gone.

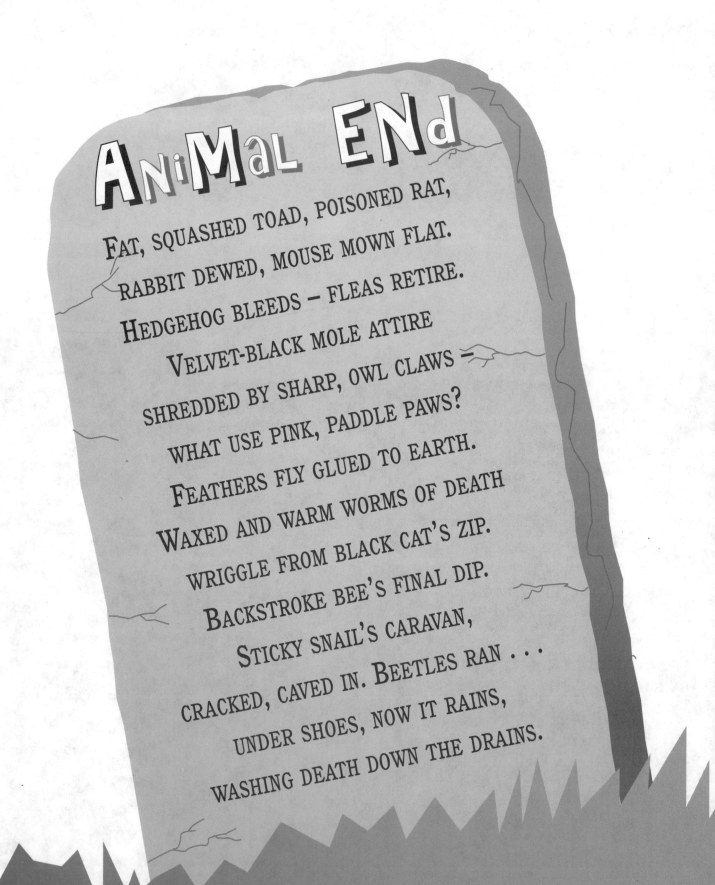

ANiMaL ENd

FAT, SQUASHED TOAD, POISONED RAT,
RABBIT DEWED, MOUSE MOWN FLAT.
HEDGEHOG BLEEDS – FLEAS RETIRE.
VELVET-BLACK MOLE ATTIRE
SHREDDED BY SHARP, OWL CLAWS –
WHAT USE PINK, PADDLE PAWS?
FEATHERS FLY GLUED TO EARTH.
WAXED AND WARM WORMS OF DEATH
WRIGGLE FROM BLACK CAT'S ZIP.
BACKSTROKE BEE'S FINAL DIP.
STICKY SNAIL'S CARAVAN,
CRACKED, CAVED IN. BEETLES RAN . . .
UNDER SHOES, NOW IT RAINS,
WASHING DEATH DOWN THE DRAINS.

Gina Douthwaite

Picture a Poem

Do houses have faces?

Should a nose be sniffed at?

Can you picture a poem?

Watch each poem leap, dance, sweep and creep its way
across the page in this brilliant collection of shape poetry!
From football to circus rings, silk knickers, rockets,
big fat men and car bonnet cats, bodies without bones
and long train delays — you'll never look at
poetry in the same way again!

£5.99
0 09 932071 1
Red Fox